Amazing Snakes!

Written by
Laura Appleton-Smith and Susan Blackaby

Laura Appleton-Smith was born and raised in Vermont and holds a degree in English from Middlebury College. Laura is a primary school teacher who has combined her talents in creative writing and her experience in early childhood education to create *Books to Remember*. Laura lives in New Hampshire with her husband, Terry.

Susan Blackaby has worked in educational publishing for over 30 years. In addition to her writing curriculum, she is the author of *Rembrandt's Hat* (Houghton Mifflin, 2002); *Cleopatra: Egypt's Last and Greatest Queen* (Sterling, 2009); *Nest, Nook, and Cranny* (Charlesbridge, 2010), winner of the 2011 Lion and the Unicorn Award for Excellence in North American Poetry; and *Brownie Groundhog and the February Fox* (Sterling, 2011). She lives in Portland, Oregon.

A Book to Remember™
Published by Flyleaf Publishing

For orders or information, contact us at **(800) 449-7006**.
Please visit our website at **www.flyleafpublishing.com**

Third Edition 9/16
Library of Congress Control Number: 2012939858
ISBN-13: 978-1-60541-146-0
Printed and bound in the USA at Worzalla Publishing, Stevens Point, WI

For Ashley, and her snake Rudy.

LAS

To the Red-Tailed Readers.

SB

What makes a snake a snake?

Snakes are reptiles.
They are in the same family
as lizards and crocodiles.

Like lizards and crocodiles,
snakes have backbones and scales,
but snakes are different because
they do not have legs.

Snakes are legless

If a snake has no legs, how can it go from here to there?

A snake uses scales on its underside
to glide in a wavelike pattern.

Can you see
the scales on
the underside
of this snake?

Can you see this snake's side-to-side track as it slithers over the sand?

Do you think a snake's skin feels slimy?

It has been said that a snake
must feel wet, like slime,
but this is not the case.
Snake scales do not feel wet at all!

6

Snakes shed their skin!

Every snake sheds its skin. When a snake sheds,
it stops eating for a day or two and hides in a safe spot.

The snake's top skin
separates from the skin
under it. The top skin splits
and the snake slithers from it.

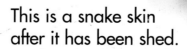

This is a snake skin
after it has been shed.

8

Can you see this snake eating an egg?

What do snakes eat?

Snakes eat animals like rats and moles.
They feed on insects and eggs, too.

Can you still
see the egg?

Snakes cannot bite or rip up what they eat,
so they must consume what they eat completely whole.

Big snake, little snake

The globe is home to over 2000 different snakes. They come in every size.

The littlest snakes are about the same length as your hand.

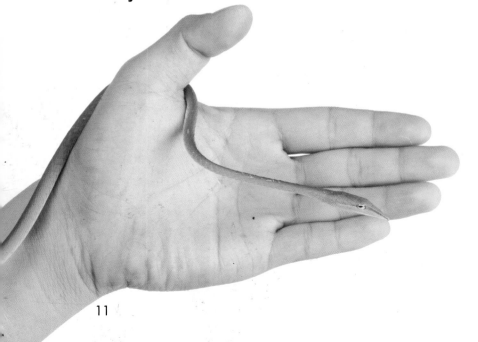

Big snakes can be as long as a truck!

Snakes and us

Lots of us do not like snakes because we think that they are slimy or that they will bite us. Snakes feel the same about us! Snakes just hope that they will be left alone.

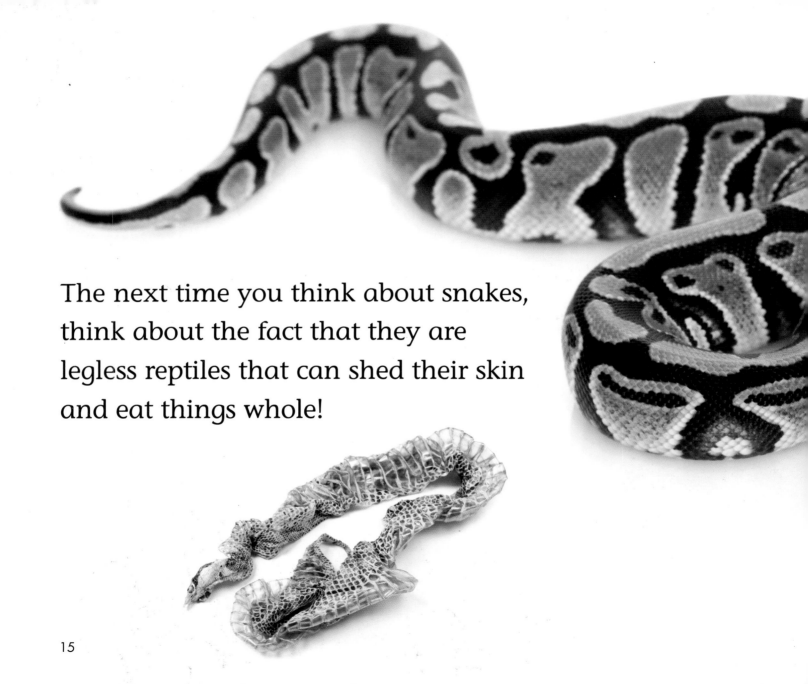

The next time you think about snakes,
think about the fact that they are
legless reptiles that can shed their skin
and eat things whole!

They can be as little as your hand
or as long as a truck!
Snakes are interesting.
In fact, they are amazing.

Prerequisite Skills

Single consonants and short vowels
Final double consonants **ff, gg, ll, nn, ss, tt, zz**
Consonant /k/ **ck**
Consonant digraphs /ng/ **ng**, **n[k]**, /th/ **th**, /hw/ **wh**
Schwa /ə/ **a, e, i, o, u**
Long /ē/ **ee, y**
r-Controlled /ûr/ **er**
Variant vowel /aw/ **al, all**
Consonant /l/ **le**
/d/ or /t/ **–ed**

Prerequisite Skills are foundational phonics skills that have been previously introduced.

Target Letter-Sound Correspondence is the letter-sound correspondence introduced in the story.

High-Frequency Puzzle Words are high-frequency irregular words.

Story Puzzle Words are irregular words that are not high frequency.

Decodable Words are words that can be decoded solely on the basis of the letter-sound correspondences or phonetic elements that have been introduced.

Target Letter-Sound Correspondence	
Long /ā/ sound spelled **a_e**	
amazing	separates
case	snake
makes	snake's
safe	snakes
same	wavelike
scales	

Target Letter-Sound Correspondence	
Long /ī/ sound spelled **i_e**	
bite	size
crocodiles	slime
glide	slimy
hides	time
like	underside
reptiles	wavelike
side	

Target Letter-Sound Correspondence	
Long /ē/ sound spelled **e_e**	
completely	here

Target Letter-Sound Correspondence	
Long /ō/ sound spelled **o_e**	
alone	home
backbones	hope
globe	moles

17

Target Letter-Sound Correspondence	Story Puzzle Words		High-Frequency Puzzle Words	
Long /o͞o/ and long /ū/ sounds spelled **u_e**	lizards	sheds	about	of
	shed	whole	are	or
consume uses			be	over
			because	said
			been	so
			come	their
			day	there
			do	they
			eat	to
			eating	too
			for	two
			from	we
			go	what
			have	you
			how	your
			no	

Decodable Words

2000	cannot	if	little	see	top
a	different	in	littlest	skin	track
after	egg	insects	long	slithers	truck
all	eggs	interesting	lots	splits	under
an	every	is	must	spot	up
and	fact	it	next	still	us
animals	family	its	not	stops	wet
as	feed	just	on	that	when
at	feel	left	pattern	the	will
big	feels	legless	rats	things	
but	hand	legs	rip	think	
can	has	length	sand	this	